T0382006

Planes

Amy Chiu and Megan Cullis

Illustrated by Bonnie Pang

Additional illustrations by Gal Weizman

Designed by Tom Lalonde and Sam Whibley

Planes consultant: Captain George Robertson

Contents

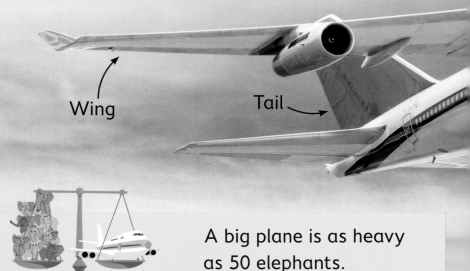

Wing

Tail

A big plane is as heavy as 50 elephants.

Sky travel

Every day, millions of people fly on planes.

There are many different types of planes, but they all have some parts that are the same.

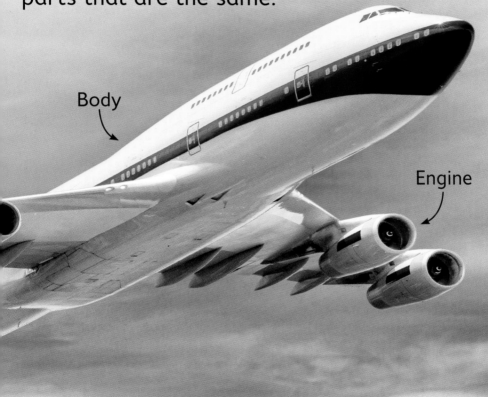

Body

Engine

This is a huge plane with room for lots of people. Early planes were very different.

Trying to fly

Since ancient times, people have tried building flying machines of different types.

Some inventors thought up machines a bit like helicopters.

Some tried gliders that swooped down but couldn't fly up.

Others tried designs with flapping wings.

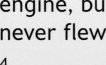

This one was powered by an engine, but it never flew.

4

The first time a person actually flew was in 1783, in a hot air balloon.

This photo shows a design with glider-like wings and an engine that turned a propeller with whirling blades. This plane didn't fly.

Propeller

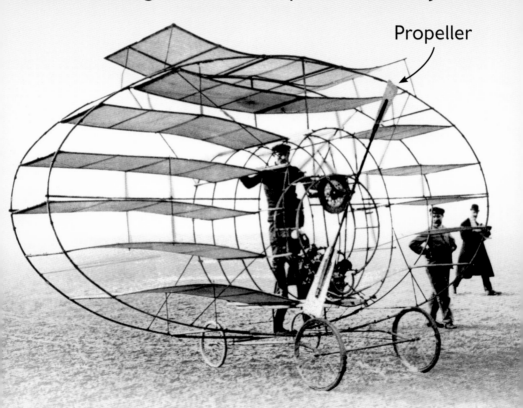

But one day a design a bit like this did work.

The first flight

In 1903, a plane flew for the first time. It was called the Wright Flyer. It was powered by an engine similar to a car engine.

Two US brothers, Orville and Wilbur Wright, built it from cloth and wood.

It had two long strong wings, fixed together with wooden supports.

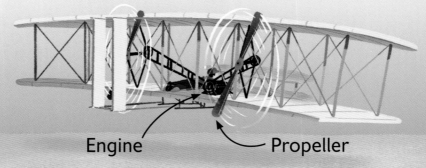

Engine   Propeller

At the back, the engine made two propellers turn, pushing the plane along and up.

6

The Wright brothers went on to design many more planes, including this one.

This is the Wright Flyer III
being flown by Orville Wright in 1905.

The Wright brothers flew one of their planes around the Statue of Liberty in New York.

Famous firsts

Soon, planes could fly further. People were excited to see just how far they could fly.

In 1930 a British pilot named Amy Johnson set off, flying alone.

She flew across the world, stopping 15 times to get fuel.

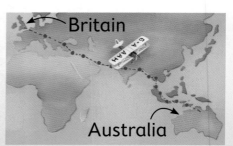

Britain

Australia

After 19 days, she landed in Australia. She was the first woman to make this epic journey.

8

In 1931, a US pilot named Wiley Post was the first to fly all the way around the world.

This is Amelia Earhart. She was the first woman to fly non-stop across the Atlantic Ocean.

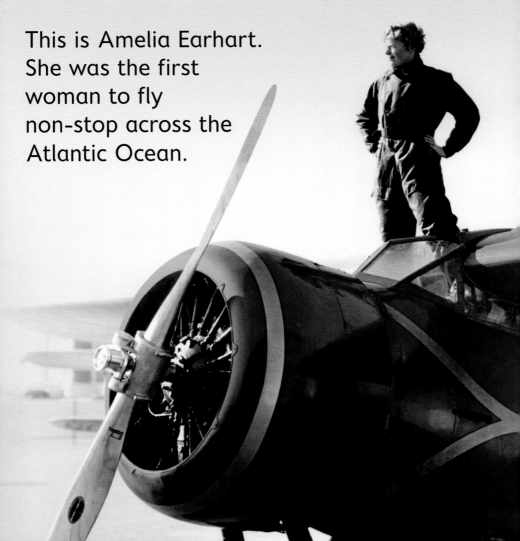

War planes

Soon, people realized that planes could help them during times of war.

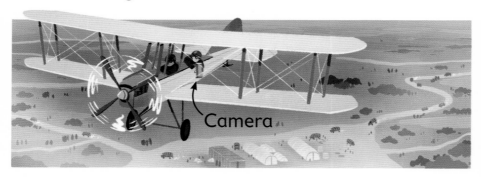

Camera

Some planes had cameras fixed to them. Soldiers flew over enemy areas and took photos to show what enemies were doing.

Parachute

Later, planes started carrying soldiers to war zones. Some soldiers jumped out in mid-air and glided down using parachutes.

From 1938, fast, powerful planes such as this Spitfire were used for fighting.

If a plane was damaged in fighting, the pilot could parachute to safety.

In 1944, Spitfires made special flights to deliver drinks to thirsty soldiers.

Amazing stunts

From the 1920s, more and more pilots did tricks, known as stunts. Crowds gathered to watch.

Some of the most popular stunts were spins and rolls...

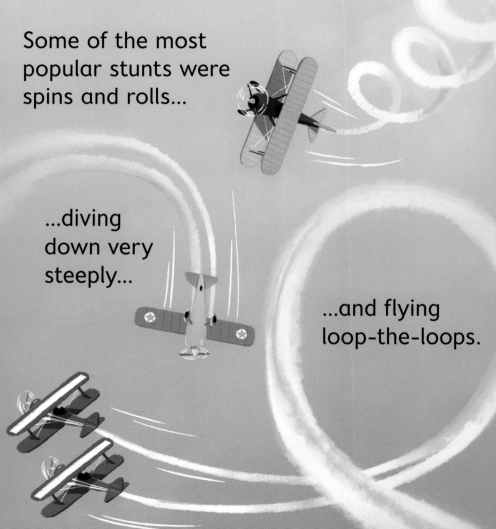

...diving down very steeply...

...and flying loop-the-loops.

People even balanced
on plane wings.
Wires held
them on safely.

One pilot managed to do 372
loop-the-loops in just an hour.

Jet-powered

Early planes all had engines that turned propellers. That changed in the 1930s, when jet engines were invented.

Jet engines made planes faster and more powerful.

Jet engine

In 1966, jet engines from a plane were fixed to a train – it set a new rail speed record.

This is an early jet plane. It was built around 1943. Now, most planes are built with jet engines.

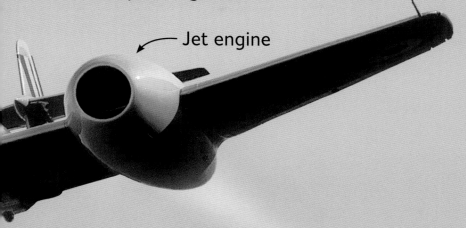

Jet engine

This is how jet engines work.

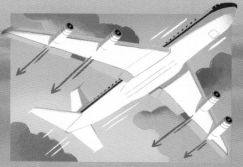

Fans suck in air. Inside, the air heats up very quickly.

Hot air rushes out the back, pushing the plane along.

Passenger planes

From 1914, small planes started to carry paying passengers. By the 1960s, passenger planes were big, fast and comfortable.

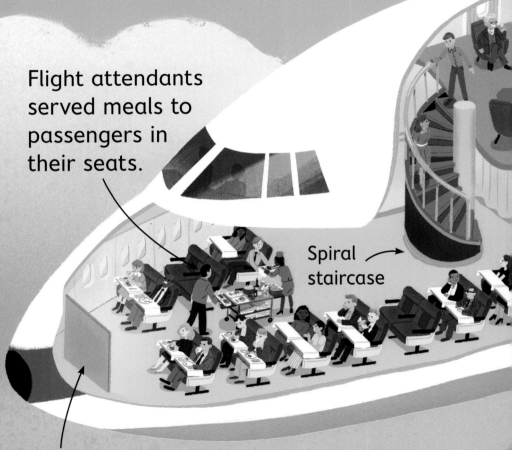

Flight attendants served meals to passengers in their seats.

Spiral staircase

Passengers watched movies on a big screen at the front of the cabin.

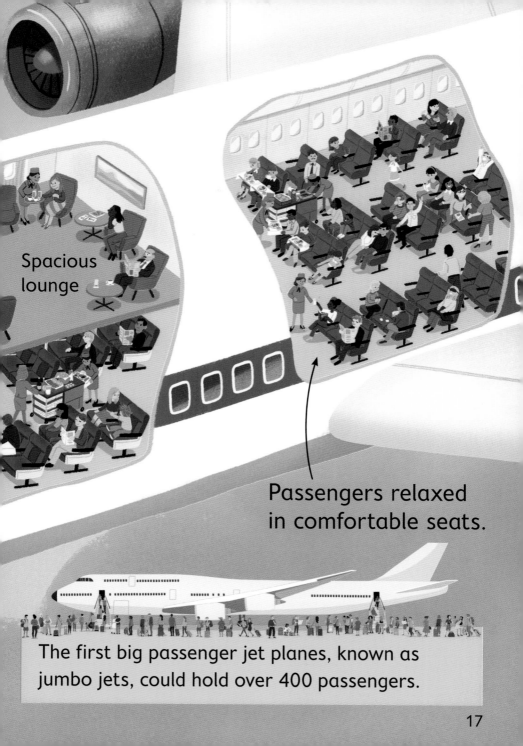

Spacious
lounge

Passengers relaxed
in comfortable seats.

The first big passenger jet planes, known as
jumbo jets, could hold over 400 passengers.

Supersonic

From 1969 to 2013, a new type of passenger plane called Concorde ruled the air. It was supersonic — faster than the speed of sound.

D-shaped wings

Concorde's nose had special features.

For taking off, the nose slid down so the pilot could see down.

Then, the nose moved up, helping Concorde fly fast.

BOOOOM

Supersonic planes make a loud noise when they pass the speed of sound.

Long, slim body

Powerful jet engines

Next, a heatproof visor slid up over the front windows.

At full speed, the nose heated up. The visor made it safe.

Planes now

Now, millions of people travel in planes each day. Planes are useful for other things, too.

Firefighting planes have big tanks filled with water or chemicals, to fight huge fires.

The plane flies over a fire and opens its tank.

Air ambulances carry doctors to treat people who are hurt or sick.

Search and rescue planes have tools to find and help people who are lost or hurt.

Cargo planes can carry almost anything — even helicopters or other aircraft.

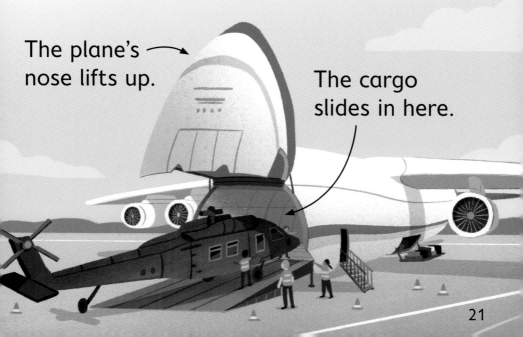

The plane's nose lifts up.

The cargo slides in here.

Flying safely

With lots of planes at busy airports, pilots need to steer clear of other planes. People called air traffic controllers help them.

Air traffic controllers work at airports in tall towers so they can see all around.

Air traffic controllers use radios to talk to pilots in planes nearby.

When a plane is ready to take off, the pilot radios to a controller.

The controller looks for a runway that can be used and tells the pilot to go there.

The pilot drives the plane to the runway, makes sure it's clear, then takes off.

At sea

Even at sea, far away from an airport, planes are able to take off and land.

Some use floating airports called aircraft carriers.

There's less space for landing than a normal airport has.

Seaplanes have floats underneath, so they can land on water.

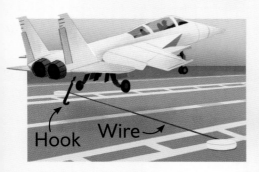

Hook Wire →

Each plane has a
hook. There are
wires on the runway.

Screeech

As a plane lands, the
hook grabs the wire.
This stops the plane.

Floats

Formation flying

Some planes fly in groups, making patterns in the sky to impress crowds for special occasions. This is called formation flying.

These planes are flying very close, but they are careful not to touch.

Planes can even fly upside down in formation.

Formation flying planes can also make bright smoke trails as they fly.

These red, white and blue trails are part of a big celebration.

What next?

Inventors are working on all sorts of ingenious ideas to help planes fly faster and use less fuel, or different types of fuel.

This shape of plane is known as a blended wing body. Slim wings join the body in smooth curves.

This shape helps the plane slip through the air easily, so it doesn't need much fuel.

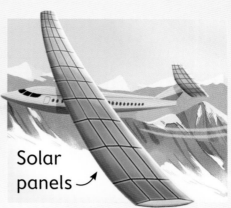

Solar panels ↗

Hypersonic planes might be able to fly 25 times as fast as the speed of sound.

Some planes could get their power from sunlight by using big solar panels.

There are already spaceplanes that go up to space like a rocket but land like a plane.

Glossary

Here are some of the words in this book you might not know. This page tells you what they mean.

 engine - a machine that provides power to push a plane up and along.

 propeller - part of a plane that spins quickly to help move the plane.

 pilot - someone who flies a plane. Pilots often work in pairs.

 parachute - a big piece of material. It helps people float to the ground.

 taking off - when a plane lifts up off the ground and into the air.

 runway - a flat place where planes can take off or land.

 cargo - the things a plane carries, from mail to helicopters.

30

Usborne Quicklinks

Would you like to watch different kinds of planes in action? Visit Usborne Quicklinks for links to websites with videos, facts and activities.

 Scan the code or go to **usborne.com/Quicklinks** and type in the keywords "**beginners planes**". Make sure you ask a grown-up before going online.

Notes for grown-ups

Please read the internet safety guidelines at Usborne Quicklinks with your child. Children should be supervised online. The websites are regularly reviewed and the links at Usborne Quicklinks are updated. Usborne Publishing is not responsible for the content or availability of external websites.

This unusual plane has a very big body for carrying extra-large cargo, such as parts for space rockets.

Index

Acknowledgements

Managing designer: Helen Edmonds
Photographic manipulation by John Russell

Photo credits
The publishers are grateful to the following for permission to reproduce material:
Cover © Daniel Karlsson; **p1** © Jon Davison/Alamy Stock Photo; **p2-3** © Paul Williams/Alamy Stock Photo;
p5 © akg-images; **p7** © SuperStock/Image Asset Management; **p9** © Granger NYC/Alamy Stock Photo;
p11 © Daniel Karlsson; **p13** © Malcolm Haines/Alamy Stock Photo; **p14-15** © Jon Davison/Alamy Stock Photo;
p18-19 © Alfredo Garcia Saz/Alamy Stock Photo; **p20** © Jose A. Bernat Bacete/Getty Images; **p22** © Markus Mainka/
Alamy Stock Photo; **p24-25** © Design Pics Inc/Alamy Stock Photo; **p26** © WoodysPhotos/Alamy Stock Photo;
p27 © True Images/Alamy Stock Photo; **p28-29** JetZero©; **p31** © Karl R. Martin/Shutterstock.

Usborne Beginners — Sun, Moon and Stars

Usborne Beginners — Farm Animals

Elizabeth I

Usborne Beginners — Rubbish & Recycling

Usborne Beginners — Dogs

Usborne Beginners — Horses & Ponies

Cats

Ancient Greeks

Spiders

Volcanoes

Usborne Beginners — Dinosaurs

Usborne Beginners — Your Body

Armour

Sharks

Usborne Beginners — The Celts

Vikings

Usborne Beginners — Castles

Usborne Beginners — How flowers grow

Usborne — Digging up the past

Usborne Beginners — Caterpillars & Butterflies

Ballet

Usborne Beginners — Pirates

EGYPTIANS

Usborne Beginners — Eggs & Chicks

Usborne Beginners — ROMANS

Weather

Usborne Beginners — Tadpoles & Frogs

Usborne Beginners — Why do we eat?

Usborne Beginners — Under the Sea

Usborne Beginners — Bears

AZTECS

Trucks
Katie Daynes
Illustrated by Christyan Fox

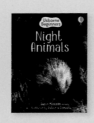
Usborne Beginners
Night Animals

Usborne Beginners
Firefighters
Katie Daynes
Illustrated by
Christyan Fox

Usborne Beginners
Antarctica
Lucy Bowman
Illustrated by Adam Stower

Usborne Beginners
Bugs
Lucy Bowman
Illustrated by Ruth Russell

COWBOYS

Usborne Beginners
PLANET EARTH
Leonie Pratt
Illustrated by Andy Tudor

Usborne Beginners
London

Usborne Beginners
Seashore

Usborne Beginners
China
Leonie Pratt

Usborne Beginners
Dangerous Animals

Usborne Beginners
Rainforests
Lucy Bowman

Usborne Beginners
Trees

Usborne Beginners
Bats
Megan Cullis
Illustrated by Carmen Mcculman

Ships

Usborne Beginners
Reptiles
Catriona Clarke
Illustrated by Emma McLennan

Usborne Beginners
Trains
Emily Bone
Illustrated by Christyan Fox

Usborne Beginners
Knights
Stephanie Turnbull
Illustrated by Ian McNee

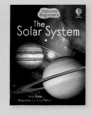
Usborne Beginners
The Solar System
Emily Bone
Illustrated by Terry Potter

Usborne Beginners
Monkeys
Lucy Bowman

Usborne Beginners
Penguins
Emily Bone
Illustrated by Jenny Cooper

Usborne Beginners
Elephants
James Maclaine
Illustrated by John Francis

Usborne Beginners
Tigers
James Maclaine
Illustrated by John Francis

Usborne Beginners
Earthquakes & Tsunamis

Usborne Beginners
Storms and Hurricanes
Emily Bone
Illustrated by Paul Weston

Usborne Beginners
BEES & WASPS
James Maclaine
Illustrated by John Francis

Usborne Beginners
Wolves
James Maclaine
Illustrated by John Francis

Usborne Beginners
Owls
Emily Bone

Usborne Beginners
Snakes
James Maclaine
Illustrated by Paul Parker